Biff and Chip had been to London with Gran.
They had some pictures which they put into a
scrapbook. They wanted to take the book to school.

Gran came into Biff's room to look at the children's scrapbook.

"We had a great time in London," said Biff. "Thank you, Gran."

Gran was pleased.

Suddenly, the magic key glowed. It was time
for an adventure. The magic took the children
into the little house. But did it take Gran?

The magic took them back in time to a street
on a foggy day. A boy was standing under a gas
lamp. He looked at the children in surprise.

"Excuse me," said Biff. "Do you know where we are?"

"Don't you know?" said the boy. "This is London."

He took his cap off. It wasn't a boy; it was a girl!

"I'm called Vicky," said the girl. "I'm called
Vicky after the queen."

"What queen?" asked Biff.

"Queen Victoria," said Vicky. "Don't you know
anything?"

"I'm hungry," said Vicky. "Have you got any money?"

"No, sorry," said the children.

"Come on, then," said Vicky. "I know where we can get some. Follow me."

They followed Vicky down winding streets.
At last, they came to a blacksmith's. The
blacksmith was looking at a horse's hoof.
The horse needed a new shoe.

"Got any jobs, mister?" asked Vicky.

"I'll give you a penny to pump the bellows,"
said the blacksmith.
The children pumped and pumped until the fire
glowed hot. It was hard work.

The children were hot and thirsty. Vicky took them to a pump and everyone had a drink. Then Vicky pumped the water and the children washed their faces.

The children were hungry. Vicky took them to
a baker's shop. She bought some bread with the
penny. She gave some to Biff, Chip and Kipper.
The bread was hot and it smelled good.

Next, Vicky took them to a street with a high
wall. A boy called Jack was waiting there. He
looked at Biff, Chip and Kipper.

"Who are they?" he asked.

"They're my new friends," she said.

They all climbed on the wall. They had to help
Kipper up. They could see a big house.

"It's Buckingham Palace," said Biff. "We saw
it when we went to London with Gran."

Suddenly, a light flashed at a window. It flashed on and off. It was flashing at Jack and Vicky. Jack had a lamp. He shone it back.

"Good," he said. "Come on, follow me!"

The children jumped off the wall and ran to
the palace.

"Keep down," called Jack, "and run fast."
Someone opened a window and they all ran
towards it.

There were three children inside. They were the grandchildren of Queen Victoria.

"They're staying with the Queen but it isn't much fun for them," said Vicky. "We come to play with them every night."

The Queen's grandchildren looked at Biff, Chip and Kipper.

"They're my new friends," said Vicky. "They've come to play tonight."

"Great, now we can have some real fun," said one of the grandchildren.

The children played together. First they played
hide and seek. Then they played tag. After that
they played hop-scotch. Biff and Chip taught
them how to play basketball.

"This is a good game," said one of the
grandchildren. "How did you learn to play it?"

"We saw it on television," said Chip.

"On what?" asked Jack.

"Oh … never mind," said Chip.

"It's fun playing in a palace," said Kipper,
"but will we see Queen Victoria?"

"I hope not," said Vicky, "we shouldn't be here."

"If the grown-ups find out, there will be trouble."
At that moment, a grown-up came in and saw
them.

"Oh no!" said everyone. "Trouble!"

The grown-ups were very cross. They were cross
with all the children.

"I told you there would be trouble," said Vicky.

The royal grandchildren were sent to bed.
A policeman came to take the others away.

"This is a serious matter," said the policeman.

"You're not allowed to play with the Queen's
grandchildren. Come along with me."

The children were taken to a police station.
They were locked up.

"You can't go home until we find your mothers
and fathers," said a policeman.

"Oh no," said Biff. "We'll be here forever."

"I don't like this adventure," said Kipper.
"It isn't much fun."
He wanted the magic key to glow, but it wouldn't.

The next day, an important man came to see the children.

"The Queen has sent for you," he said. "Come with me."

The policeman let them out.

The important man took them to Buckingham
Palace.

"Do you think we are going to have our heads
chopped off?" said Kipper.

Gran was having tea with Queen Victoria.

"Gran!" said Chip. "What are you doing in our adventure?"

"I'm having an adventure of my own," said Gran.

Queen Victoria looked at all the children and smiled.

"Your grandmother has told me that you are good children," she said. "You can play with my grandchildren and stay to tea."

The children played in the throne room. They
had a sack race.

"Come on Biff," called Gran.

"Come on Vicky," called the Queen.

"This is fun," everyone said.

"You can have one more race," said the Queen, "and then it will be time for tea. I hope you like scones and home-made strawberry jam."

The magic key began to glow. It was time for
the adventure to end.

"Goodbye," said Kipper. "Thank you for
having us."

"It was a pleasure," said Queen Victoria,
"do come again."